LOVE, TASTE AND BLOOD

VIGNESH RAMANATHAN

ISBN 979-888546972-2

Hello all. Its been a long time. This is Vignesh Ramanathan and I am here with my third book. My second work in Notion press. I dedicate this book to my family, friends and everyone who is reading this book. I hope everyone loves it.

Contents

Foreword

In this book, I have used reference from my real life and the movies I have seen. I would like to thank those movie makers which helped me to imagine something beyond human limits. I think I will be successful in taking you with me in this journey while reading this book.

Preface

Hello all. I was inspired to write this story while I was watching Walking dead. How good the man is, at some point to survive he may take some selfish decision. The decision we make during our critical situation decides who we are. Whether we are good or evil.

My previous two books are romance, this book also have romance but it also deals with some other interesting subjects. I think you will get lots of unexpected moments in this book.

Prologue

Chapters

CHAPTER ONE

Tinder world

After returning from Mahabaleshwar, my routine life started. Basically I am from Madurai but I stay here in Chennai, I work here in an IT company. My parents are in Madurai. My day to day life is the same everyday. Wake up, get ready, catch the cab, login, work, lunch break, work, meet the boss, return, I have been doing this for the past three years.

I have got two friends in this office world. Let me introduce them to you. Rohan, he is a North Indian from Kolkata, he joined with me in this office and then a malayali girl Aishwarya. I still remember the day she joined the team. Entire men were behind her. Till now, lots of guys are behind her. She got married recently but still I have to agree that most women say " All men are the same."

It was lunch time, I was still working at my desk. They both came near me and Aishwarya locked my screen.

She said " Come Yoga. It's time to take some rest. "

Rohan made fun of me by saying " Are you planning to become the director of this office immediately? Working so hard."

I replied " It's not like that. I have been on leave for the past three days. If I don't work today, Hitler will shout at me."

We named our boss as Hitler. Rohan is his favorite, he gets scolded by him each day. He too has some feelings for Aishwarya.

She said " Ok guys, let's go for lunch."

Our gang went to the cafeteria. They both bring food from home regularly for me. I asked " What's special today? "

Aishu said, " I brought sambar rice with beetroot."

I was disappointed and said " I should have never made a vegetarian girl as my friend."

She got angry and said " Then find a non vegetarian girl and ask her to join our gang."

Rohan said " No. Have you seen world movies? Each gang must have only three members. Not more than that. "

I asked " Why so? "

He answered, " When the crowd is more, the least entertaining guy might feel lonely."

Aishu smiled and said " Then it will be your Yoga."

I said " No, I never felt lonely."

Rohan interrupted " You are addicted to loneliness man. Travelling alone to different places. You are turning into a loner. "

Suddenly I remembered about the weird thing that happened in Mahabaleshwar.

" Guys I want to talk to you about something? "

Aishu predicted " I think you are going to tell your travel to Mahabaleshwar story."

I said " Yes. But something strange."

Rohan was very eager to listen to the story.

I started " A tea shopkeeper suggested a place named Rani beef centre." As soon as I mentioned beef, Aishu's face changed.

" I went to that place and had a dish named " Rani special", which consisted of beef fry, chicken leg piece fry, fork fry, gravies of chicken, pork, duck, mutton, beef and rice. Then there was an egg which was filled with blood. I tried all the items and each tasted great. I was flying in heaven while eating it. I never had drugs but I felt like I was having drugs. It gave a similar kind of feel. While eating the blood fry, I saw a beautiful lady in red saree. As soon as I completed it, she vanished. They mentioned that it was that lady's blood which I had. When I heard it I fainted. I woke up in my hotel room. I went back to the same place again. But whatever I saw before was not there. When I asked the people nearby, they told various stories. One thing was true, there is no Rani beef centre now. I don't know whether I really had that food or it was just a dream."

Rohan was impressed by this story and started clapping. He said " You turned out to be a great story teller."

Aishu said " It might be your dream Yoga. You are always alone. You might get these kinds of dreams as long as you are alone."

Rohan said " Yes, she is right." He opened his lunch box and it was egg fried rice.

I took it and said " At Least you brought non vegetarian today."

" Don't try to change the topic." Aishu shouted.

She said, " Find a girl."

Rohan said " You yourself find him a girl. Introduce him to your friends."

She said " All my friends are either committed or married. We have to wait for their breakup or divorce. It's a long process."

Rohan said " I have a better idea. "

I asked " What's that?"

He replied with excitement " Tinder."

I said " I don't have enough money to pay for tinder. And I am not interested in a relationship."

Rohan said " Who is asking you to be in a serious relationship? "

Aishu hit him and said " You are spoiling him with poor ideas."

I was eating the egg rice which Rohan brought. Suddenly I was not feeling the taste of it.

I asked Rohan to try the food. He said, " It's tasting the same."

" I can't taste its taste."

Aishu gave her food and said " Try this."

I ate it and it was the same. I couldn't feel the taste of it.

I nodded my head, signalling that I couldn't taste the food.

She said " Once you reach home, please visit any nearby doctor."

I said " Okay. Don't know why this is happening."

Rohan asked " Do you think it's related to your weird dream? "

I was confused at that time and said " I am not sure."

Aishu said " It happened once to my husband. He automatically recovered. It's not a big issue. Don't overthink. And it's not related to your weird dream. Then don't forget to install the tinder app."

At the end of the day, I returned home and took my phone to install that dating app.

" Oh my god! It's 500 rupees per month."

I created my profile and started swiping it. The Tinder world was new for me. It showed me lots of girls. Most of them were very attractive. I liked the profiles which matched slightly with my interests.

I lived in this tinder world for almost 6 months. I met lots of girls and went out with them to different places. But my taste bud issue continued. Just like going on dates with the girls I connect with on tinder, I was visiting the doctors regularly for this issue. Even they failed to find a solution. One day, I had a date with a girl who is also a doctor.

We met in a Starbucks coffee shop in VR mall. She came in a red frock. When I saw her, I was shocked. It reminded me of Rani, the girl who appeared when I was in Mahabaleshwar. She was looking exactly like her.

When she came towards me, I stood up and said " Rani."

She smiled and said " You mean queen. I am not a queen. I am the devil."

She said it as a joke and took her seat. She asked " Shall we order something? What would you like to have? "

I was staring at her. I was completely frozen. It is her. The same lady whom I saw.

She said " Hello, are you here? "

I suddenly reacted to her and said " Anything you wish. I had some issues with the taste bud. Whatever I eat will be the same for me."

She asked " Is it? I am a doctor, I think I can help you. I will ask someone from my clinic to deliver you a tonic. Have it before eating, the issue will be resolved."

" Thank you" That's all I was able to tell her.

She ordered some flavor of coffee. We were having it and had a casual chat.

She asked " The age which you mentioned on tinder. Is that real? "

" Yes"

" Ok. I am older than you then. "

" I know."

She asked " What else do you know? "

Suddenly her visuals from that dream appeared in my head. I lost my focus.

" What happened to Yoga? "

I was quite disturbed and said " Sorry, I am a little nervous."

She said " That's fine."

I started drinking the coffee. I couldn't feel the taste.

Then after some time, we left that place. She dropped me at home in her car. I was sitting with fear. I had lots of questions running in my head.

" Who is she? Is she the same person? Does she know about me? Is she a ghost? How can I meet a woman whom I met in my dream? How did I have no idea of that woman when I saw her on tinder but was able to recognise her when she appeared in front of me? Did I see the same woman on tinder? " Lots of questions were running in my head that night.

CHAPTER TWO

Life of Yoga

It was a beautiful monsoon weather in Mahabaleshwar. I was riding my rented bike in the hills. I saw a giant elephant crossing the path when I was travelling in the forest zone. I waited till that elephant crossed the path. One question raised in my mind " How good it will be to fry an elephant's lungs and eat it? " I never tried it. But I wish to do it once in my life. The elephant cleared the path. Now it's my turn to reach the hills. In between the journey, I found a tea shop. Eknath, a marathi old man was the owner of that shop. I stopped and placed my bike near his shop. There was no one except him in that shop. It was like he just now opened the shop. He was arranging everything.

I asked, " Bhaiya. Can I get a cup of Chai?"

He was washing the utensils and said " Yes. Please take your seat. "

There was a bench made of wood in which five members could be seated. I sat there and started waiting for the tea. I was tired as well so it was a perfect time for me to rest. Tamasha, it's my favorite bollywood movie. I thought of hearing the " Agar tum saath ho" song in the meantime.

Eknath asked " Babu. What's your name? "

I paused the song and answered " Yoga. Full name Yogeshwar, from Tamilnadu. "

He was happy when I said Tamilnadu and he said " Actually, my daughter is married to a Tamil guy from Madurai. She went there to study MBBS, she fell in love with a guy. I accepted since I cannot say no to my daughter's wish. "

I was quite happy to hear that story and said " Wow, it's great to see such a progressive man in this forest area. Even the city people are not very progressive. "

He said with pride " Yoga beta, I have read lots of books in the government library which is in my village. I read books by Ambedkar a lot. So I don't see differences based on caste, religion, language etc. "

The tea was ready. I was very happy talking to this old man. He gave me tea. I played the song and started drinking the tea. It suddenly started raining. The combination was great " Hill, surrounded with trees and grasses, a cup of tea, rain and agar tum saath ho song". It was a pure blissful moment.

Eknath asked " Are you on a tour? "

I replied " Yes I am on a tour but a food tour. "

He was aware of its meaning and said " Oh I have seen it on TV and YouTube. People visit different shops and post their experiences about the foods and shops. "

I said " Absolutely. If you are okay, shall I post something about your shop as well? "

He refused with a shy " No beta. But I can recommend a place. It's just two Kilometer from here. The shop's name is Rani Beef center. The Buffalo roast will be great. People come from different places to try it. Even foreigners love it. First of all, do you eat beef? "

I answered " I am a food addict. I am ready to eat whatever they make from the flesh. Please tell me the route uncle. "

I completed the tea and told me the route to the shop. The rain too stopped. I started my journey to that shop.

The roads were very steep so I stopped my bike and started walking. In 20 minutes I reached the spot. The roads were wet because of the monsoon weather. The shop was visible with colorful lights in the display board " Rani beef center". I felt like watching a bollywood movie set. Almost 20 to 30 people were seated. The shop was too busy. I saw Buffaloes, cows, bulls, porks, goats etc being kept in the farm. I saw two men asking for deer soup.

A thin guy who was standing in the soup counter said " Sorry, we don't have deer soup here. It's illegal. All we have is mutton soup and chicken soup. If you want I can bring you beef or pork soup. "

One of the two guys replied " Who wants the regular soups? Life is good only when we try different items to eat. "

The guy turned towards me and asked " Am I right brother? "

I didn't know what to answer and just said " Yes."

They both left the place. The soup counter guy said " These morons are always asking for something different. Where will I go for deer soup? "

I sat at a table in which two men were eating. One's plate was filled with mutton chopsticks and the other guy was having beef biryani it seems.

Waiter walked towards me and asked " What would you like to have sir? "

He asked me that question in English and I gave my orders " I want something that is related to Buffalo. "

He said " Buffalo omelette will be better. "

I was surprised and asked " Do Buffalo's lay eggs? "

People who heard it started laughing.

A guy who was eating said " No brother. It's a chicken's egg only. They break the egg and add the masala needed for omelette, over the layer they add the boneless Buffalo fried pieces and over that they add their beef gravy. It gives a wonderful taste to that omelette. "

I was impressed with the way he mentioned the recipe. I ordered the same.

He asked, " Anything else sir."

I was searching for something in the menu card. It mentioned " Rani special ". It was the most costliest among all the foods available in the menu.

I ordered it. He took the order and left. I was wondering what it would be. It took almost thirty minutes to bring the order. The shop was too busy. Lots of orders came, the cooking continued, the waiters were serving too fast. Finally my order arrived. Everyone in the crowd saw my ordered food jaw open.

The plate was filled with rice, chapati, sweet, then gravies of each animal they had in the farm, fried pieces of each animal. Then there was something which was placed in between boiled eggs. It looked like a goat's blood fry. But it was kept in a low quantity. I was sure that I cannot complete it alone. So I asked the company " Who would like to join me? "

No one came forward.

One guy said " It's a tradition here. We don't share Rani special. You must complete it all on your own. You must complete that egg and blood combo. "

I agreed to the challenge and accepted their tradition. I started eating the food. The gravies tasted extraordinary. It was different from the one which was added in the Buffalo omelette which I tasted simultaneously. Suddenly I felt like my stomach was very happy. I was flying through Mars in my imagination. Entire men in the shop were happily watching me eat. The taste was something beyond universe. Suddenly I heard footsteps clearly. A woman came out of the kitchen. She was wearing a red saree, loose hair and bindi on her forehead. She was very traditional. She was watching me eat. She was very beautiful. After I finished eating, she suddenly vanished. I was shocked and shouted " Who was that woman? "

One man said " It's Rani. She will come once you taste her blood. She will go once it is completed. "

I was terribly shocked and said " What? Did I eat her blood?"

I fainted there. Suddenly when I woke up, I was in my hotel room.

I was still feeling the taste of the food I had. I took my bike and went back to the same shop but I couldn't find the same shop. There was a Punjabi Dhaba.

The tea shop was also not available. I enquired with the nearby people.

Some said " The tea shop has been closed for almost a year. "

When I asked about Rani beef center, people gave strange and weird answers. But the common answer I got was that it was completely burnt because they served beef, the locals here considered cows as their holy god. Some people say they killed a man and to get rid of the murder, they cut him into pieces and made it into a gravy and served people.

Another horrible statement I got was people who dream of eating in Rani beef centre, end up dead by accident or nature. The reason for the death will be their taste buds. I was thinking how can a person's taste bud kill a person.

On the other end, my mind was telling, this is just a village. There will be lots of rumours and superstitious beliefs here. So I thought of ignoring those and returned to Chennai.

CHAPTER THREE

My Ola driver

I was sitting at my office desk thinking about Rani. I checked my tinder account to see the details of the last person I met. There were no details of her. I was shocked and went to meet Aishwarya.

She was busy working. I stood behind her. She turned and asked " What happened? You look so nervous."

" It's happening again." I said with a fear in my face.

I explained to her whatever happened yesterday. She checked my phone and tinder account.

She couldn't find anything and said " It's your dream Yoga. The best thing you can do is ask Rohan to stay with you for some days."

I said " Don't know why I am getting these kinds of weird dreams. I will check with Rohan whether he can stay with me for a few days. "

I was confused when I was explaining my situation to Aishu. Then I went back to my bay. I had some pieces of paper in my pocket. I threw it in the dust bin.

(Yoga didn't notice that there was Starbucks coffee shop bill in his pocket which he threw in the dust bin)

I was working a little slower than usual these days. Lots of things were running in my head.

Aishu came to my desk and asked " Are you not leaving? "

I said " I haven't completed my work yet. I will extend it for sometime. "

She said " Ok. Take care. How is your taste bud issue? "

" It's still the same."

She said " I don't know what to suggest for this. I will take a leave. Bye."

" Bye."

She left. I was alone in my bay. The evening was dark today. Suddenly I could sense the smell of some non vegetarian food. It was the same smell which I got when I had Rani special food.

I heard some noise from the cafeteria. I was afraid. I walked towards the noise with fear. There was no one and I was able to find a plate with the same dish I saw in Rani beef centre. I screamed and started running from there. I took the stairs and went down. I was breathing harder.

I was searching for security. He was not available as well. Suddenly he appeared in front of me. I asked " Where have you been?"

He answered " I went to smoke. Please don't tell anyone."

Then I booked a cab through the ola app. Someone accepted it and it was a lady driver. Her name was Nisha. This is the first time I am seeing a lady cab driver. I took the screenshot and sent it to Rohan. So I can make sure whether this is a dream or reality.

The cab arrived. She was checking her phone to confirm whether the customer was me. I went near the cab and said " I am the one who booked the cab."

She asked " May I know the OTP? "

I checked my phone and said " 0506 ".

She opened the lock of the door. I entered the cab. I was feeling something strange but I don't know what that feeling is.

The cab started

While driving, she asked " Have you marked the exact location of the drop? "

" Yes. If you get any doubt in route you can ask me."

" Ok sir."

I started checking my phone. I didn't receive any messages in whatsapp, Instagram or Facebook. Then I checked my mail. I got some new offers from Naukri. She played a song in the cab. The song she played was " Paarthen '' From Power Paandi, a tamil movie.

I asked " Could you please raise the volume?"

She raised the volume of the speaker and asked " Do you like this song? "

" Yes. This is my favorite song."

She happily replied " It's the favorite song as well."

" That's cool. It was shot in my native place."

She asked " Are you from Madurai? "

" Yes. How did you get it? "

She explained " You said that this song was shot in your hometown. That's why. I am from the same town as well."

" Is it? "

She asked " Do you know Rekha sweets shop? "

I knew that shop and said " Haan. It is near my home. The owner Srinivasan uncle is very well known. His daughter is Rekha and he kept her name."

She said " Actually he has two daughters. The younger one completed her studies staying here in Chennai."

" Is it? I never knew he had a younger daughter. I visited Madurai only on holidays. That might be the reason. How do you know them? " I asked.

" His younger daughter is me. My name is Nisha."

" Oh sorry. That's great to hear. We are neighbors but have never seen each other. This is common in Chennai but I can't believe that we haven't seen each other in our village. "

She said " Even I can't believe it."

Suddenly the cab stopped on an empty dark road. There was no one nearby.

I asked " What happened? "

She said " Don't know. I will just check and let you know. "

" Shall I call the mechanic? "

She angrily said " What do you think about me? I can do it myself."

She took her kits to check the car.

I was looking at what she was doing. Suddenly I heard a weird sound.

" Did you hear it? "

" What?" She asked it with no idea about that sound.

" I heard something strange."

" Don't try to prank me. Please."

She thought I was joking. I heard it again. But she had no idea of any sound. My life has lots of suspense and surprises waiting for me these days.

She called me " Excuse me. I need your help."

" Yes."

She gave me a torchlight and said " Please hold this. I will clear everything."

I was holding the light and she was repairing the car. Again I heard the sound.

" Don't you hear anything? "

She said " No."

She repaired the car and then we went inside. The cab started again.

I said " Never seen a female cab driver and I was amazed when you repaired the car by yourself."

She asked, " Can we do these things? "

I answered " I never said you can't do this. I just said, I have never seen this. " You are something special."

She said " There's nothing special. I just did what others do."

" Okay."

I was feeling sleepy. I tried to sleep. Suddenly, I felt someone was sitting next to me when I looked in the mirror. I turned left and found Rani. She was wearing the same costume she wore when she met me in the VR mall.

I shouted " Aaah."

But Nisha didn't react. She was just driving the cab. She had no idea what was happening behind her.

Rani said " She can't hear anything or feel anything. She will be just driving. "

I was afraid of her and asked " Are you a ghost?"

She smiled and said " What else would I be?"

" What do you want from me? "

She took a tonic from her pocket and said " I don't need anything from you. You needed something to cure your taste buds. This will help you."

I was surprised and asked " So you want to help me? But why?"

She said " I will need your help one day. Just give and take policy."

" Oh got it. What help is that?"

She suddenly vanished. Then I woke up. I thought I had a little dream. But when I checked my pocket I found the tonic bottle she gave me.

Nisha asked " Had a tight sleep? "

" Yeah. I was a little tired."

" That's okay. We have reached your destination. You can sleep well."

" Thank you."

I got down and paid her for the cab ride and said " Nice to meet someone from the same town."

" Yes. Hope we meet again." She said,

I smiled. Then she left. I went inside my room. I had lots of questions regarding Rani in my head. I tried to check her medicine. So I had a biscuit without that tonic and I was not able to feel anything. Then I took that tonic and had the biscuit. Now I was able to feel the taste. The medicine worked.

CHAPTER FOUR

Thirsty crew and dance

I started taking that medicine every time before taking that food. I couldn't find any medicine for that. The bottle didn't have any label on it. So I was not able to find what it was. The next day in the office was quite interesting.

I was having lunch with Rohan and Aishu. She brought Malabar vegetable biryani. I had it and said " Wow! The taste is amazing."

She was surprised and asked " Has your taste bud started working?"

" Yes."

Rohan said with excitement " Wow dude! Your buds started working at the right time."

Aishu had no idea what he was talking about and asked " What are you talking about? "

He said " We are having a client party coming weekend with a thirsty crew. It's a dance party. We might have alcohol as well. More important, beautiful girls and foreign ladies might arrive."

" That's cool." I said.

Aishu said, " All men are the same."

I said " Agreed."

I talked about the girl whom I met as a cab driver.

Rohan asked " Did you get her number? How was she? "

I said " She was beautiful and I didn't get her number."

He also said " You didn't get Rani's number as well."

I explained, " She was just a ghost."

Aishu said, " Stop it. No more horror stories while eating."

I continued, " She gave me the medicine as well."

Rohan said " So you're telling me that she gave you the disease first and then she gave you the medicine."

" I am not sure whether she gave me the disease or not. But there is a reason why she gave me the medicine. She said it's a give and take policy." As soon as I completed my explanation, Aishu and Rohan started laughing. They considered this as a joke. They never took the topic of Rani seriously.

That night, I was sitting alone in my room. I was craving to eat something non-vegetarian. I searched for grilled chicken in Zomato. I ordered it.

Then I checked my phone everyday. There were no messages. I spent 30 minutes doing nothing. Simply wasting time like the other millennials on Instagram, Facebook and Twitter. My order arrived.

I opened it and had it without taking the medicine. I couldn't feel the taste. So I took the medicine and had it. While eating, I felt like someone was sitting behind me.

I was sure that it was Rani.

" Rani" I said softly with a doubt.

She appeared in front of me and said " Nowadays you are not afraid of me."

I replied " Because I don't feel you are dangerous. You give me a feeling of a friendly ghost these days."

She shouted " Aah"

Suddenly, the room lights turned off and on.

She asked " Aren't you afraid now?"

I replied " No. Do you want some chicken? "

She answered " I don't eat these things. I prefer something else."

I asked " What is that?"

She calmly said " You would get to know soon."

Then she vanished. She always comes like a Vedalam from Vikramaditya story and leaves a question in my head.

Even after finishing the grilled chicken, I was still hungry. My hunger for non vegetarian food continued.

Two days later, it was the client party day. We were asked to come directly to the Thirsty crew. It's a restaurant with a bar in it. I wore my Jean shirt and casual pants, then a matching shoe. I reached the spot. Rohan was waiting for me there.

He raised his hands and said " Come on dude. Don't know how many girls are going to fall for you tonight."

I laughed.

I watched the entrance of the building and asked " Shall we go inside?"

He said " Aishu will be arriving with her husband. Just wait for a few minutes."

" Okay."

We were waiting for her. There was another gang going inside. I saw Nisha with that gang. She didn't notice me.

I said to Rohan " This is the same girl whom I saw as the cab driver."

Rohan said " Oh cab driver. God is playing with you man. You got an opportunity to meet you again. This time I got her number. Try to become her friend."

I just ignored his words. Then, Aishu and her husband arrived.

She introduced us to her husband. Then we all went inside.

In the meeting, they were talking a lot. We felt bored. Aishu and her husband went separately. Me and Rohan started eating. I filled my plates with non vegetarian foods.

Rohan said " Dude, at least eat some vegetarian food."

I said, " Who the hell eats vegetarian at a party like this."

Then I started eating it. I was feeling like I haven't eaten any non vegetarian food for almost years. Suddenly someone touched my shoulder from behind. I turned back. It was Nisha. She was looking very beautiful in this party dress.

" Remember me?"

She asked it with a smile on her face. I had no words in my mouth. Rohan kicked me from behind.

I said " Yes. How are you?"

" I am fine. Hanging out with my friends. What about you?"

" It's an office party."

It was dance time. Everyone started dancing.

She asked " Would you like to dance with me?"

I answered happily, " Yes."

Rohan from behind said " Lucky guy."

Me and Nisha started dancing. The first song they played was from Ok Kanmani.

" Mana mana mental manadhil."

She asked " Do you like watching movies?"

I was dancing and answering her questions.

" Yes. Movies and food are my life."

She continued.

" What's your opinion on living together? "

" Nothing wrong with it. If you love someone, I don't think you need cultural rituals to prove it and make it strong."

I think she was convinced with my answer.

" What's your opinion on Nayanthara? She had two boyfriends and now she is in relationship with a new guy."

" Nothing wrong. Not everyone finds the right one in the first attempt itself. People say love happens only once. It's a false statement. Nothing wrong in breaking a relationship if it's not working out.'

She was dancing and said " That's great."

She asked lots of questions about indian culture, feminism, relationship etc. I hope I was giving the answer she was expecting from me. Rohan gave me a signal to get her number.

I was a little nervous to ask for it, but suddenly she herself asked me for my number. I gave her my number.

She said " I will call or text once I reach home. If you are free please respond to it."

" Sure. I will do it."

Then she left. The party was almost over. Most people left the place. I was sitting alone in a table. Rohan sat nearby.

I asked " Where is Aishu?"

He answered " She went with her husband. She was looking for you but you were busy with Nisha."

" Kk"

He said " Finally, God sent a girl into your life. You have been searching for lots of girls on tinder."

I smiled. That night I went to my room and texted her.

" Hi."

I got the reply as " Hey."

The chat continued the entire night.

CHAPTER FIVE

Singing under the moonlight

I was in my kitchen doing some cooking. I was cutting onions, tomatoes, ginger, garlic etc to make biryani. I ordered chicken from the delicious app which arrived. While preparing it, the smell was very attractive. It attracted my neighbour. He stood and watched me cooking through the window. I saw him as well.

He asked " Are you cooking biryani inside?"

" Yes."

" Shall I join you this afternoon for lunch?"

He asked it and I was ready to invite him. Because there was no one else to complete this biryani. I didn't even know his name. All I know that he is my neighbour.

After an hour, I completed my cooking. As soon as the cooking was finished, the neighbour knocked on my door.

Opened the door and then he came with excitement.

" Where is the biryani?" He was searching everywhere.

" I found it."

He entered the kitchen and brought the biryani to the hall. I brought the plates.

I asked " What is your name? "

" Rishikesh."

He opened the vessel and smelled biryani. I distributed the biryani to each other.

He said " I am alone in my home but have never cooked non vegetarian food. I always eat only hotel foods or cook vegetarian food at home. Never tried chicken at home. I might not cook the chicken well. That's why. Will you teach me how to make biryani?"

" Sure."

We both started eating biryani. He said " Biryani is extraordinary."

He saw the medicine which I took before eating and asked " What is that?"

I answered " I have some issues with my taste buds. I can taste foods only after taking that medicine."

He said " That's a weird disease. Never heard about it."

I said " Life teaches us a lot in each stage. Get ready to learn."

He laughed and said " I don't know why you said this at this moment but I like it."

Then we completed the biryani and washed the plates and vessel. There are two dogs always roaming outside my room. We gave some pieces of rice to them. They ate it happily.

That night while chatting, Nisha asked me " Shall we go for a movie?"

I was excited and said " Sure."

She said " Normally I watch movies alone in the theatre. You said you love movies, that's why I asked you."

I pinged " Yes I am ready. May I know which movie?"

She texted " Aamis."

I googled about that movie and found that it was about cannibalism. I felt a little nervous and started sweating.

I replied " Ok I am coming. Which theatre? "

" Pvr at VR mall."

" Okay."

Then she said good night and I went to bed.

Next morning in the office I was talking about this to Rohan.

He said " Everything is happening too fast, man."

I replied " It's because we are kind of neighbours in my hometown. Otherwise, this wouldn't have happened."

He pinched me and said " You are a lucky guy. Meet her in a decent costume."

" Okay."

" Then don't tell her about Rani."

" Haha." I laughed. But I suddenly thought it's been a long time since Rani appeared.

In the restroom, I was washing my face. Suddenly, Rani appeared in the mirror.

She said " Long time no see."

I replied " Don't know why ghosts do the same prank. Don't you know other kinds of entries? "

" We do know what you know. Nothing else."

I said " Oh no! Another riddle. Whenever you give me something which makes me think a lot. I am going to ignore your points."

She said " I have nothing to lose." She said it again, " I have nothing to lose."

Then she disappeared. I was disturbed again.

Finally the day arrived, I went to VR mall. This is the mall where I met Rani first. I had the medicine which she gave me. It's almost half now. It will be over soon. Don't know when she will be providing the next bottle.

I called Nisha and asked " Where are you? "

" I will be coming in ten minutes."

" Ok. I will be waiting for the Chai kings."

" Okay."

I was sitting in Chai kings and ordered a tea. I saw what was happening in the mall. It was filled with family and friends. There was a boy and girl playing the walking dead shooting game. I think they are meeting after a long time. Then someone from behind said " Hey handsome, would you like to go for a movie with me?"

It was Nisha. I stood up and said " Hi. Do you want some tea?"

She said " Who says no for tea. Let's have it."

We had tea and left for the theatre. While walking to Pvr, there was a biryani shop which displayed their varieties of biryani. My mind said " Eat it all. Eat it all." I felt like someone was talking to me. It was something strange.

She bought the ticket and then we entered the Audi 6 to watch the movie. Lots of advertisements were running before the start of the movie.

She said " The thing I hate the most in Pvr is that they display lots of advertisements."

I said " I hate that too. Shall I buy popcorn?"

She said " Okay."

" Anything for you?"

" No. We can share the popcorn."

Then I went outside to the cafeteria and bought popcorn and a cold coffee combo. When I entered the audi 6 again, it was completely dark. They turned off the light before the start of the movie. I had a huge smell of blood and flesh. I felt like smelling 100 dead bodies. But they all were alive.

I went to my seat and asked " Can you smell something weird?"

She took the popcorn and said " No. Whenever we meet, you ask these kinds of questions. Last time you were asking, did you hear something and now you are asking about smell."

I said " I had some strange feelings. "

She replied " I don't know why you get these strange feelings when you are with me."

Her statement raised the same question in my head. The movie started and we were watching the movie silently eating the popcorn. The movie was also about a foodie who falls in love with a doctor. She is already married as well. During the intermission, I asked " Do you need something?"

" Already my stomach is full. There is no place in it."

" Ok. I feel the same. Let's eat something once the movie is completed."

" Okay."

After a few minutes, the movie started. The ending of the movie was completely surprising. I never expected this kind of ending in the film.

After completing the movie, we both went to Urban Spatula for dinner.

I said " This is one of my favorite restaurants. Butterfly prawn is the best."

She asked " Butterfly? "

I explained " It's prawn made like KFC chicken. They will provide you with mayonnaise and sauce as the dip."

She replied " But I don't like mayonnaise."

I said " Then I will eat it, you just watch it." She hit Me on my shoulder. We completed our dinner. Then it was dark. We came out and walking in the streets of Anna Nagar.

Suddenly I heard the same sound which I heard when I first met Nisha.

I said " Rani."

She appeared in front of me. Everything else paused. Nisha was like a statue. I was shocked.

I asked " What happened? "

She answered " Just a simple trick which I can do. I wanted to talk to you."

" Regarding."

" Give and take policy." She mentioned.

I said " Yes. The medicine is about to end. Please give me some more."

She said " You have it with you." Then she vanished. Everything turned normal. Again she gave a hint and left.

Nisha asked " Why do you look weird? Have you seen any ghosts?"

I said " Don't know. Never walked with a girl in this street at this time."

" Okay." She asked, " Shall we sing a song together?"

I asked " Which song?"

" Paarthen song from power paandi." She smiled and replied.

We both were singing that song in the dark road and walking. Rani was watching us from behind. We both had no idea about it.

CHAPTER SIX

Brownies

I was sleeping happily and peacefully this weekend. Suddenly someone knocked on the door. I woke up angrily to open the door. I thought it was my neighbour. But surprisingly, it was Rohan and Aishu.

They both shouted " Surprise."

I too shouted " What a surprise?"

Aishu stared and said " Nowadays you don't have enough time for us."

Rohan said " He is committed these days. You too did the same Aishu when you were committed."

I interrupted " Excuse me, who said we are in love. We haven't proposed to each other yet. We are just friends as of now."

Aishu pointed " As of now. Mark this point."

I asked " Suddenly you people came. I don't have anything here to serve you."

Rohan said " You don't need to serve anything to us. I brought the ingredients to make the brownie cake."

I said " Brownie. What is that? "

Aishu said " Even I don't know. He saw it in some restaurant and then he saw a YouTube channel for recipes. Now he is torturing us to make brownie."

" Ok let's start the work." Rohan said and left for the kitchen.

As soon as he started the booking. I saw the neighbour Rishi watching us through the window. He called me outside, signalling through the window. I went out and asked " Tell brother. What is the matter?"

" What are you cooking today?"

" Brownie."

Even he didn't have any idea about it. He said " What is that? "

I answered " It's a kind of cake. I will bring it to you once we prepare it."

" Ok Yoga."

Then I went inside my room. We were helping Rohan to make the brownie he was making.

I saw the cake he was making and asked " Is this really brownie?"

He stared at me. Aishu started laughing. I too joined her and laughed. He got irritated and threw my taste bud medicine at us. The bottle broke and the medicine was wasted.

I shouted " Oh no. That's my taste bud medicine."

Aishu said " You escaped from tasting the brownie which he is going to make."

Rohan said " Sorry dood."

Aishu looked closely at the medicine and said " It looks like human blood. Is this really medicine? "

I said " Yes."

Rohan said " Ok. I will clean it up. Take care of the cake."

I took the broken glasses and Rohan cleaned the floor. Aishu received a call from her husband. She was talking to him. I too felt the same. It looked like human blood. I asked " Shall I order something non vegetarian?"

Rohan said " Vegetarian or non vegetarian. You will feel the same dude. Your buds won't work without the medicine."

I was sad and said " I feel like eating chicken tandoori."

" Nothing can be done. If you want you can order it. After we leave you can visit the doctor and ask for medicine."

He was right. I need to check with Rani for the medicine. I need to get it at any cost.

Then the cake was finally ready. He brought the cake and said " Look at my masterpiece. How is it looking? "

Aishu said " The shit you cook is shit."

I said, " That's a great Breaking Bad reference."

I tasted it and couldn't feel anything. He said " It's ok dood. I can understand."

Then Aishu tried it and said " Wow! You are such a talented man."

I was surprised and said " Really! "

Rohan raised his collar and said " I think I need to leave the job and start a brownie shop."

Aishu said " This is too much."

Then we had those brownies. Even though I couldn't taste it, I had it. We had some fun chatting inside the room. Then we played video games and watched the Sri Lankan premier League. Aishu was very much interested in archery. So she saw the recent Olympic match in which India won. The day ended happily. They both left. I gave some brownies to Rishikesh, my neighbour. He tasted it and appreciated it.

Then I went inside my room and I was still craving for meat. The hunger rose each hour. I shouted " Rani."

She appeared.

" Hey handsome."

I asked " May I get that medicine? "

She replied " I already told you. The medicine is with you. Find it." She gave the clue and vanished.

I had no idea what she was taking. I was thinking about the series of events which happened. At some moment, I felt like Nisha is the medicine. But how is that possible? Then I remembered Aishu telling me that the medicine looks like blood. So I tried to experiment with my blood. I ordered Tandoori chicken, Mutton soup and Fish Tikka. Waited for an hour. I was feeling more hungry than ever now. The food delivery came. I opened the parcel. Then I took a blade and cut my finger. I sucked a drop of blood and stopped the blood with a cotton sponge.

Then I started eating the food. I was able to feel the taste. My blood was the medicine. Rani appeared next to me.

She said " So you found the solution."

I replied " The answer is my blood. "

She corrected " It's just blood. It can be anybody's. How long will you be relying on your blood alone? "

I asked with a doubt " What are you telling? How long will this continue? "

She answered, " Until I get what I need from you."

She vanished. I shouted " Rani. What the hell do you want from me? Please give me my taste back."

I was really frustrated. I don't know what to do next. I was checking for Rohan's brownie. The vessel was empty. I wanted to taste brownies. So I pinged Nisha to come to Anna nagar the next day evening.

Next evening, she came to meet me in Anna nagar.

She asked " Why suddenly Anna Nagar?"

I said, " Let's eat brownies."

She said " That's all."

I said " Yes. That's all."

She said with a disappointed face " I thought it was something else."

" What?"

She angrily said " Nothing. Let's go and eat some brownies." We started walking. There was a shop named Brownie studio. We went inside and ordered brownies. Then I left the restroom and tasted my blood.

Then we both had the brownies. She looked disappointed.

I asked " Why are you so dull?"

She said " Haven't you understood anything?"

" No. What?"

She angrily said " Should I openly say that I love you? "

I was happy and said " If you love someone you have to tell them openly. Just like I am in love with you."

She said " Okay."

We both then continued the brownies and a little chat. I knew that she wanted me to propose to her. I was waiting for the right moment to propose to her.

Then we were walking back to the cab she booked. I said, " A cab driver is booking a cab." She smiled and said, " That's the worst joke."

She said " Do you know something? I don't like brownies."

I asked " Then why did you eat it?"

She replied, " To give company."

" Oh. Thank you. But you can tell if you don't like it. I won't take it bad. "

" Ok."

She entered the cab and was looking at me.

I shouted " Hey beautiful girl. What's your name? "

She answered " Nisha."

" May I get your phone number? "

She said " Yes. It's 9998880506."

And then I could not control myself and said " You look too beautiful. I love you."

She didn't say anything and started smiling and called my number and said " Do you think you are Alai Payudhey Madhavan? "

I said " Yes."

Finally I proposed to her and she said yes. I was walking the street happily.

(Rani was watching all this drama. Her voice " Everything is happening as per my prediction."

CHAPTER SEVEN

Living

Next day at the office, I was happily roaming. Rohan saw it and asked " Hey man. You look so happy today. What's the matter?"

I replied, " I proposed to Nisha and she accepted it."

Rohan shouted " That's great news. You must give me a treat. Today Aishu is also on leave, so you must buy me biryani in the canteen."

I agreed. We went to the canteen and bought biryani. He had it. I tried to eat but I could not taste. I forgot to collect the blood.

He figured the issue and asked " Same issue? "

" Yes."

He said " Chicken biryani is wonderful. You must definitely taste it. You missed the taste."

He was tempting me very much. I went to the restroom and pinched my finger with a pin and sucked the blood. I heard Rani's voice " How long?"

I ignored that voice and went back to the canteen. I was feeling like the whole world was shaking.

Rohan asked " Are you okay?"

" Yeah I am fine."

I started eating the biryani and it tasted very good. I ate like I haven't had biryani before. It was very abnormal.

Rohan asked " What happened man? You are eating like you haven't been a vegetarian for the past ten years."

I stopped and said " I am very hungry today."

He replied " Yes when you are happy, you will be more happy. Enjoy the food."

We both completed the biryani and went for the second round. Rohan was shocked.

He said " I know that you are a foodie but I have never seen you eating like this."

" I don't know man."

" Sometimes I feel like the Rani story which you told us is real. I am very afraid, man." He was a little worried.

I said " No dude. It was just a dream. It's not related. I am a little hungry today that's why."

" Ok."

We went back to our respective desks and started doing our work.

My love life was going very smoothly. We went out every weekend. We explored new restaurants and foods each weekend. We went to every superstar movie. Recently we visited the book fair and I bought a Ponniyin Selvan book collection for her. One day we went to the Vgp marine kingdom and then we visited the snow kingdom. We did a photoshoot in ECR beach. Then finally we decided to go to Pondicherry and have a candle light dinner at a French restaurant.

Nisha brought her friend's car to travel to Pondicherry. I was ready and went towards her.

She asked, " Would you like to drive the car?"

I said " No. You drive."

" Why? "

I casually said " Because I don't know how to drive."

" Just a car or a bike too? "

I said " Bike too. I ride easily on empty roads but I am afraid of crowds and traffic."

" But why?"

" I don't know. I am always afraid of crowds. I feel lost in a crowd. I don't even attend marriage functions or friends gatherings if there are more than three people. I feel lonely when the group is bigger."

" Why do you feel like that?"

I said " Because I will be the least important person. If there are three people, I will be third most important, if four I will be fourth, if hundred I will be hundredth. I will be ignored and forgotten in that big group. I even tried not to go to the thirsty crew but Rohan forced me. That's where I met you again and the story of life changed."

She smiled and said " That's a good finish to a saddest story."

We started our trip to Pondicherry. While driving, she asked " Yoga, do you have a past?"

" Yes. But I won't talk about it."

" Why?"

" Past is past. We have to just move on. Even if I tell my story it will feel like a made up story. And I don't want that to happen. "

She heard everything and said " You are a man of mystery. "

I asked her to turn on the radio. She turned it on. It was " Ooh solriya mama, ooh ooh solriya mama" Song. I started enjoying it and started dancing. She too shakes her shoulder.

The Pondicherry trip was very exciting. We had our breakfast in a local shop on the highway. Then, we booked a room in Auroville. Had a visit to Auroville and in the evening, we reached Pondicherry French colony. I saw the famous Patti kadai fish bajji shop.

I asked Nisha to try this. She bought a fish bajji and a prawn bajji. It was actually a street food shop but very famous because of food reviews. Even foreigners and North Indians preferred it.

We both started eating the bajji. Nisha's face changed when she had the fish bajji.

I asked " What happened?"

She said, " It's horrible."

I took the small bottle in which I filled my blood and had a sip of it.

Then I tasted the bajji and I even found it horrible. Then we moved from that shop.

Then we went to the beach. I was sitting with her and watching the beach. Suddenly the smell which I got in Pvr while watching Aamis movie came. It was the smell of flesh and blood. Whenever a person crosses me, I smell it. It was very strange. Definitely it is Rani's work. She is behind this. Right now I can't call her. Suddenly Nisha pinched me.

She asked " What are you thinking about? "

I said " Tonight. Will we book two separate rooms or a single room? "

She said " Single room."

I too said " Yeah that's perfect."

" Why?"

I said " Budget will be saved. Two rooms might cost more."

She hit me and said " So you are worried about the room budget."

The day was almost over. We took some selfies. Later we reached the French cuisine where we planned our candle light dinner. It was on a rooftop. We had a lot of privacy there.

It was almost dark and just the moonlight and the candle light.

She gave me the menu and said " Hey food expert. Look at the menu and order something."

I said, " You order by yourself."

She looked at the menu and started laughing. I asked " What happened?"

She said " The dish name looks funny."

" What's that?"

She said, " Buffalo omelette."

I was shocked when she mentioned it. It's the same dish which I ordered along with a Rani special dish. My face suddenly changed.

She asked " What happened? "

I said " Nothing. It's an omelette which has layers of Buffalo meat."

She didn't like it and said " I will skip it."

Then we ordered a chili prawn, red wine lamb meat, peri peri chicken, mushroom masala and Naan. It was a great feast. Suddenly I felt like the whole building was shaking and Nisha was sitting like nothing was happening.

Rani appeared after a long time. She said " Missed me? "

I was a little upset and said " What do you want? Why are you here? "

She said " Nowadays you are ignoring me a lot. That's because of your girlfriend. She is very beautiful."

" Yes she is. But why are you here? "

" She has beautiful flesh and blood. It will be very nice to have Nisha fry, Nisha grill, Nisha fried rice etc." She continued irritating me.

" Stop it."

I shouted with irritation. Suddenly she disappeared. Nisha asked " What happened? Are you dreaming?"

I said, " Nothing."

She was eating the food very happily. But my mind was filled with whatever Rani told. Suddenly I was able to feel her blood flowing. I felt like craving to eat her flesh. I was trying to change my mind but I couldn't. I tried hard and behaved normally.

The dinner was completed. They arranged a music program. We both loved it.

Nisha suddenly asked me a surprising question.

" Shall we live together, Yoga?"

I asked " Why?"

She replied " To save rent. Hey you fool. I want to live with you."

I said " I was just joking. Yes you can."

Suddenly I had an inner voice telling me " That's a great decision, Yoga that's great."

Then we went to our room. It was a private villa. She asked " Shall we sleep on the same bed?"

I said " No."

" Trying to become a gentleman?"

" No. I may be out of control today." I refused because I felt like I may bite her.

" Okay. Then you can sleep on the sofa. I will sleep in the bed. Else, if you want a bed there is a bed in the other bedroom. "

" That's fine. I will sleep on the sofa."

She said " Good night."

" Good night. "

I turned off the light and slept on the sofa. She slept in the bed. Suddenly, I heard someone laughing and it was definitely her. I am not afraid of her anymore. Just afraid of myself.

CHAPTER EIGHT

Flesh And Blood

Rohan and Aishu were shocked when I told them that me and Nisha are planning to live together.

Aishu asked, " Really?"

Rohan couldn't believe it and said " I can't believe man. You are getting into a commitment too early."

I said " No it's not a commitment. We will be living together. That's all. She will be doing her day to day work and I will be doing mine."

Rohan asked, " What about that part?"

I didn't get that and asked " What part?"

Even Aishu couldn't understand what he was talking about.

Rahul said " You people don't have enough knowledge to understand this. I am leaving the restroom."

After a few days, Nisha moved into my room with her luggage. I carried some of her luggage and Rishikesh helped us in carrying some.

I introduced him as " This is Rishikesh. My neighbour. Whenever I cook something, he will be the first person to try it."

She smiled and Rishi continued the chat " Actually that's the power of his cooking. He is a great cook. Especially non vegetarian foods, he is a master chef in it. Even if I am in my bathroom, I can smell his cooking. It attracts me directly here."

She said, " That's good to hear." Then he left. We entered our room and sat on the sofa.

She said " Room is nice."

I said " I clean this room everyday. That's why."

" You can cook, you clean rooms, you work, you wash clothes, all you have been doing alone."

" These are essentials, Nisha. I have to do it. Just like we eat, we need to clean, wash etc. It's a part of day to day life."

She said " That's right."

She lied on the bed and said " I will take some rest. Please prepare something for me."

" Sure."

I planned to prepare butterfly prawns which I had in Urban Spatula. I saw the recipe on YouTube and left the shop to buy the ingredients which I needed.

Then I started cooking it. Suddenly I felt more hungry. Little unconscious as well. I took my blood. Rani appeared inside my head.

She asked " How long will you be drinking your own blood?"

" It's all because of you."

" It is not time to blame me. It's time to find the solution."

I asked " You know what's the solution. Please tell me."

She laughed and said " I know the solution. But it's too hard. All I can say is you will feel it more if you drink your blood more. Find alternate ways."

Then she left. I didn't completely understand what she said. All I felt was my blood causing this craving and unconsciousness. I looked at Nisha. I felt like a tiger watching a deer. I was feeling like I was waiting to hunt her.

Something inside was controlling me.

After preparing the dish, I woke her up.

She asked " What's special? "

I said, " Find it yourself."

She came to the dining table. She saw butterfly prawn and then rice and mushroom gravy. She said " That's nice."

We both started eating. She enjoyed it very much. There was some food left.

She asked " My stomach is full. Too much food is left. "

I said " Don't worry. There are three people who share this. I will fill some in a box and give it to Rishi."

" Other two?"

" Two street dogs always visit my house. I will give it to them."

" If food is not wasted, I am happy."

Then I cleaned everything. She helped me in cleaning everything. Then I packed food in a tiffin box and gave it to Rishi. Gave other leftovers to the dogs.

That night while sleeping, I was very hungry. I couldn't control it. I saw Nisha sleeping. Without disturbing her I went out of the house.

I took my bike and found the road was empty. So I can drive peacefully. As I said before, I can't drive well when the road is full of vehicles. In Mahabaleshwar, I drove beautifully since the road was empty. While travelling I was searching for shops to eat. It was almost midnight so there was no shop. Suddenly, Rani appeared behind me. She was with me on a bike. I stopped and asked " What are you doing? "

She asked " Why are you wasting time here when you have food available at home?"

" Stop this nonsense."

She said " She is the only solution to fulfill your hunger completely."

I said " No I can't do that. Please suggest something else. "

" Other flesh can solve your problem temporarily but she is the only one who can put an end to it completely."

I said " Oh shit. I am completely frustrated."

Then she left. I found a midnight dhaba.

I ordered a full grilled chicken and had it. But still my hunger continued. I went back home. I was hungry and felt unconscious. I was sure that Rani was telling me to eat Nisha. Her flesh and blood is the solution for my hunger but I can't do that. She trusts me. Then I decided to cut some muscles from my leg and try it. I took a knife and cut some muscles from my thigh part and stopped the bleeding. I fried the thigh part with some masalas added. It was frying very well. Then I had it. The taste was very awesome and addictive. I felt like I needed more of it. The hunger stopped. I was normal. But I still remember what Rani told. This is just a temporary solution. I cannot cut my muscles everyday to stop my hunger. I need to find some alternative solution.

Then I slept on the floor. I felt satisfied but there was little pain in my leg. Rani appeared and slept next to me. She asked " From where did you get this idea? Cutting your own muscles."

I said " It's from the movie which I watched with Nisha. The movie's name is Aamis. It's an assamese movie. In which the guy cooks his own muscle and gives it to the woman whom he loves to impress her."

After listening to this statement, she left.

After a few days, I felt the same. There was no one at home. I tried to cut the thigh muscle from the next leg. I did it and cooked. I felt normal again. I was thinking " How long will I be doing the same? I need to find an alternate solution."

I was thinking about what to do. Then I think of getting help from a local gangster who can help me in getting human flesh from anywhere.

I got details from a councillor's son who is my friend. Then I visited the gangster at his house. He was just three years older than me with a clean shave.

He was alone at home. He asked " Would you like to have some water?"

" Yes."

He asked " What's the matter?"

I said " It's a simple job. I need human flesh."

He asked " Human flesh. Whose flesh do you need?"

" It can be anyone's."

He was confused and asked " What will you do with that?"

I explained to him a lie " It's for dark rituals. My house is haunted and I can't leave it. Then I met a fortune teller, she said to conduct a ritual with human flesh. Everything will be fine."

He asked " Do you believe her? "

I replied, " I didn't have any other option."

He agreed and said " Ok. I will do it."

" How much will it cost?"

" Rs. 50000"

" That's too much."

He said " It's not chicken or mutton. Its human flesh. I need to get it from my friends who are involved in murder. You might turn into an evidence if that murder is found. That's why we need to be careful while doing this."

I was a little afraid while doing this but I can't risk Nisha for my hunger and I cannot stay without her. So u gave 50000 rupees and agreed to whatever he told.

I was in the office working. I received a phone call from Ravi, the gangster whom I arranged.

He said, " The flesh is ready."

I told him that I will come directly to his place. I had to make some arrangements before taking it home.

I reached the place where he asked me to come. It was a dark building.

I asked " Whose body is that? "

He refused to answer it and asked " What's your next plan? "

I said, " I need to get rid of the bones."

I stretched a plastic cover so no blood is wasted and if it spreads it might cause some trouble. I took a knife and started cutting into smaller chicken pieces. Ravi was watching me weird. He doubted that it's definitely not for rituals. I cut that body into boneless fleshes. I filled it in a carry bag and kept it in my bag.

I asked " Do you have any car? We need to avoid the smell till I reach home."

" I will make an arrangement for that."

He called someone and brought the car. I took it in the car and reached home. I googled how to get rid of the smell.

It mentioned I need to clean it with vinegar and water. I followed the same. There was not enough vinegar, so I bought additional vinegar from a nearby shop. I cooked some flesh and then washed the other fleshes and kept it in the freezer.

Surprisingly, Nisha arrived early today.

I was shocked. She didn't notice. She asked " Are you cooking?"

" Yes, it's almost completed. You came too early."

" Yes. I had a little headache. I haven't eaten anything. Did you make additional food or just for you?"

I didn't know how to tell her no. She came to the kitchen. The bowl was full. So she assumed that both people could eat.

She said " This is enough for both of us."

I tried to stop her from eating this by saying " This is Buffalo meat. You won't eat it. "

She said " Who said? I will eat."

" The taste might be horrible. I am trying this for the first time."

" That's fine. Let me taste it."

She tasted it. She was impressed and said " It is an extraordinary dish. The best dish I ever tried."

I served her. The taste was really amazing. She was very happy while eating it.

She said " Make this Buffalo gravy regularly. I love it man."

" Sure. "

She had no idea that it was human flesh gravy. After finishing the food, she said " I would like to kiss the chef who made it."

I went near her and said " I am ready. "

She kissed me. I had flesh in my refrigerator which I can cook for next one week.

CHAPTER NINE

Orgasmic death

I didn't know what to do with the other flesh. I started cooking different recipes with that flesh. One day I tried it as tikka, then in kfc style, then barbeque and one day I even tried applying honey. Nisha thought it was Buffalo meat and started enjoying it. She too joined me in cooking and we both tried different recipes.

Once I made biryani with that flesh. I took it with me to the office. Aishu is a vegetarian so didn't touch it.

Rohan was loving the biryani and said " It's awesome man."

" I did it with the help of Nisha."

" That's great. Is this beef biryani?"

" Yes dood."

I didn't want to inform him that it was human flesh.

Aishu asked " Your taste buds are working fine right?".

I said " Yes."

Finally, I cooked sixty five with the remaining human flesh. We all finished it fully. I don't know where I will go next.

After a few days of not eating human flesh, I felt the same feelings again. I was very hungry and felt unconscious. I fainted suddenly in my room.

Nisha saw that and ran towards me. She poured some water on my face. I woke up.

She asked " Are you alright? "

I said " Yes. I will take some rest."

' okay."

After Nisha left for work. I locked the door and went to meet Ravi at his place.

When I met him, he was sure that I am here for human flesh.

Ravi said " I know that you are here for human flesh and definitely it's not for rituals. I need to know the truth."

I am sure that I cannot lie to him.

I said " It's for cooking. I love to eat human flesh."

He vomited when I told him about it.

He said " That's disgusting. Is that really tasty?"

I said " You will love it man. Do you want to try?"

He said " No."

I said " I will pay you 50000 again."

He agreed for money. I asked " Why don't you try?"

He said " No. I won't. You do whatever you want. All I need is money."

After two days, I didn't receive any response from him. I gave him an advance of Rs. 20000.

I went in search of him. One of his men said " He has been missing for the past two days. Maybe he is hiding from the police."

I was slightly afraid because if he gets caught for any reason I may be caught as well.

But that was my secondary headache. Primary one was what am I going to do about my cravings for human flesh. Even Rani is not appearing these days. She said that the flesh of Nisha can cure me permanently. But how will I get her flesh? I cannot kill her to cure me.

Then I visited a mortuary. I saw a man who looked very innocent. I brought him separately.

I asked " Can you do me a favor? I will give you money."

He said " What favor? "

" I need a dead body."

He refused, " Sorry sir, we cannot provide that."

I forced him " I will give you as much as you want. "

" Sorry sir. I cannot take this risk for money. If you stay here for long, I will complain about you."

Then I left that place.

I was roaming in the streets with a hungry stomach. I tried eating lots of food but still it didn't stop. I followed my traditional style of cutting my thigh muscle and fried it. I had it for two days. I survived with the help of it for the next few days. Nisha figured out that something was wrong with me.

She asked " Are you alright? "

" I don't know Nisha. Something is killing me. I feel like dying."

She had tears in her eyes and said " Wait. I will call the doctor."

I never wanted to tell her the truth of what was happening in my life. Then a doctor came. Surprisingly the doctor was Rani. I was not able to move my body or take any action.

She checked my body and said " He is having some internal problem."

Nisha asked, " What kind of problem is the doctor?"

" He is craving for something. No matter how much medicine he takes in, when he gets the perfect medicine. He will be alright."

Nisha asked, " Do we have any cure?"

She said " Yes. I will give you some medicines which will cure him temporarily as of now. I will provide the permanent medicine later. "

" Ok doctor."

She gave some medicines to Nisha and left. She turned and gave a smile looking into my eyes.

Nisha gave me some medicine and she took care of me. I was feeling good.

I woke up from bed.

She asked " How are you feeling now? "

" I am fine now."

She said " It's been a long time. We spoke a lot. Shall we go out? "

I said " Yes."

" Let's go to Perambur Park."

I asked " Why Perambur park?"

" I like ice cream which is sold next to that park."

I said " Then ok. Let's go."

While going to the park, something was running in my head. It was saying " Eat her, eat her, eat her. She can cure you completely."

I was very disturbed because of that voice. We spent some time together in the park.

She asked, " Shall we get married?"

I was shocked because she asked it very casually. I just said " Yes."

She said " Let's celebrate it with ice cream."

" What about your parents? "

She said " I will take care of them. You take care of your parents."

I said " Okay."

She loved vanilla flavour and I loved chocolate flavored ice cream. Then we returned to our room happily.

I took permission from my parents and they agreed for marriage. The same happened at Nisha's home. They decided on our marriage. But we stopped our living relationship. She went to Madurai and I stayed in Chennai in my room.

After a week, the medicine which Rani gave turned empty. I didn't know where to get another piece of flesh. I called Rani. She appeared.

" Why are you torturing me Rani?"

" I am not torturing you. You are torturing yourself."

" Please give me a cure."

She said " I already gave you. It's Nisha. Her little flesh can solve your issue."

" Little flesh."

She said " Yes. You don't need to kill her. Her little flesh will help you."

Then she vanished. Now I started thinking how I will get that little flesh from her.

CHAPTER TEN

The End Of The World

I invited my friends Aishu and Rohan to my wedding.

They both hugged me. Aishu said " I am very happy for you man."

Rohan said " Another member from this three idiots crew is getting married. And I definitely need a bachelor party. "

I said " Sure."

Aishu saw the invitation and said " So the marriage is in Madurai."

" Yes."

Rohan happily said " We will come for sure man. Don't worry."

When I went back to my room, I saw it was open. I felt something was wrong. There was a gun on my table and found a letter below it. I took the letter and read it. It was from Ravi.

" Hey, this is Ravi. Police is searching for me. If I get caught I will never tell you. You need to help me in return. This gun belongs to me and I did something with it. If the police find that gun, it will be evidence and they will punish me for lifetime. So hide that gun somewhere until I come. Because that gun is very important to me. I didn't know whom to trust with this. If I gave this to anyone else, the police would have easily smelled. This gun is very important to me. You were the only person I was able to trust. I need to hunt down someone with that gun. So please keep it safe."

I read it and felt like another problem was added to my problem checklist. I kept it inside a table. No one is going to come here anyway.

But I still had the issues with my cravings and unconsciousness. I was managing it by cutting some flesh from my body. One day, the cravings were too much. So I decided to search for another gangster in Ravi's area who might help me in getting flesh.

I was searching for someone related to Ravi. I found a man whom I saw with him.

He saw me and stopped. He said, " Sir I don't know where Ravi is."

" I am not here for him."

" What do you want from me sir?"

" I need human flesh. I will give you money."

He said " I don't have flesh but I know someone who recently killed a man. They can give you some flesh. I will talk to them regarding this."

" Okay."

Then he took his phone and spoke with someone.

He completed the call and said " Sir, they will give only one hand to you. They will place it in a bag near that auto which you can see from here." He pointed to an auto.

" You give the money to me and collect it from the auto."

I was waiting for people to place the parcel in the auto. Few men arrived and placed the flesh in the auto. Then I gave Rs. 20000 to him and left. I took the parcel and left that place.

Next day, I started preparing chettinad style food with that flesh.

The television was turned on by me and in the news channel they talked about the area which I visited yesterday. The hand belongs to a person and that man was killed yesterday by the local goons. Police also stated that one hand is missing. I saw that hand frying in the kitchen.

I remembered one dialogue in Tamil " Konna paavam, thinna pochu."

The people who gave me flesh are arrested and the other one is hiding from the police. Don't know how I am going to survive from now on.

For two months, I was controlling myself. One day I decided to visit a nearby cemetery at night and steal a dead body from there. But when I went there, there were already few men doing the same. One of them saw me. So I started running. They started chasing me. I started running as fast as I could. Then I hid on the rooftop of a home. They were tired so they went back. For a moment I felt like there were lots of people like me in this world.

I came back the next night, this time the cemetery was empty. No one was available. I checked the soil to find which was recently buried and I found a place to dig. I dug it without anyone noticing. I was shocked because the body which I found belonged to a small girl. She must be 10 years old. But I was very hungry on one side and on the other side, I was not able to do it. I heard some sound so I left the body and ran from that place.

Finally it was my marriage day. Everything was new for me. Lots of people roaming here and there. Aishu and Rohan arrived.

Nisha came to see me in my make up room.

She locked the door and said " It's been a long time. Since we saw each other."

" Yes."

When she came near me, I felt like biting her like a vampire. But I stayed in control.

She asked " Why are you so nervous? "

I joked, " This is the first time I am getting married."

She laughed and said " Worst joke"

" Why are you here?"

She came closer and said " I need a kiss."

I kissed her on her cheek and she said " I need it in lips."

" Nope I can't do that."

She said " I am your wife. Won't you give it to me."

She forced me for a kiss and I kissed her on the lips. I felt like eating flesh and I bit her lips. She said " Ouch."

I said " Sorry. Sorry."

She was angry and said " You must see lots of Kamal Hasan films and learn how to kiss." She opened the door and went to her room.

At last I got married and every formality was completed. Then we had our lunch together. I was not able to taste it. She fed me with some food. The photographer took photos of us. We gave our latest wedding photography poses. After marriage, we had some traditions to follow. They arranged for our first night in our village itself. I was afraid of it because of the cravings I have.

At our first night room, she herself said " I am feeling very tired, shall we have this some other day? "

She told me exactly what I had in my mind.

" I too felt the same."

We both slept after hearing Ilayaraja and Yuvan shankar raja song together in a single headset.

After few days

We came back to Chennai to our room. Now it has turned into a family room. We made lots of changes and bought some more essential items.

She said " This is the place where we are going to start our life as husband and wife."

I said, " We already lived together here."

She said " But it was before this knot was tied."

" A knot cannot decide my love towards you. Even if you rejected my proposal, I would have still loved you. "

She was impressed. She hugged me which tempted me.

Since she was on break from her job, she was mostly at home. So I was not able to arrange for flesh. My condition was very bad. Whenever I see Nisha, I feel like eating her. One evening she sat beside me and asked " Can you have that Buffalo meat once again?"

" Why?"

She said " The taste was very addictive. I want more of it."

" I will try to get it."

She begged and said " I will do anything for it. Please please get it for me."

I felt like she was turning just like me. To check her I asked " Do you know Rani?"

She asked " Who is Rani?"

From her expression, I found that she doesn't know about Rani.

I said " She is a goddess. People worship her with Buffalo meat in Maharashtra."

She said " Is it? Never heard about it."

I was thinking about how to get rid of this disease. I felt like " Shall I ask Nisha to give some of her flesh to me? " But on the other hand, I felt like what she will think about me when she knows the truth that I did so much.

Days passed, and at one stage I decided to cut some of her muscles without her knowledge. So I bought Anaesthesia illegally. Then I hid it behind the television.

This is going to be the strangest night in one man's life. Never seen a husband trying to eat wife's flesh. That night, we had dinner early and she slept. I was waiting for her to sleep. This is the perfect time to inject her and get the flesh I need to cure my disease.

I felt like this is the end of the world.

CHAPTER ELEVEN

WTF?

I took the injection and I was walking slowly towards her. Rani appeared after several days and said " Finally I am here to see the moment I was waiting to witness."

I ignored her and walked slowly. My heart was beating faster than usual. My Whole body was sweating. I went near her. Nisha woke up and she caught me carrying an injection. She woke up immediately and said " What are you trying to do?"

My heart almost stopped and I knew that I can't hide anything from her. Another shocking surprise was her next question.

She asked " Who is this lady? Is she the doctor?"

I asked " Are you able to see her?"

" Yes I can. But what are you trying to do?" She shouted with fear.

Rani said " Complete the job you started Yoga."

I shouted " Stop it."

Nisha was afraid and said " Are you trying to kill me Yoga? "

" No. I want to confess something to you."

Rani from the other end shouted " It's not time to confess. It's time to cut her flesh."

Nisha got scared when she heard these words from Rani. She tried to run. But I pulled her back and pushed towards the table and the lock of the table opened.

Nisha was hurt and she looked at me. I said " Nisha, just ignore and listen to me. She is not a lady, she is a ghost. If you don't trust me there is a gun on the table, take it and shoot her. She won't react to it."

She said " Gun. What the hell is a gun doing at your table? "

She took the gun and spotted me and said " Who the hell are you? Are you a gangster? Are you a psycho serial killer? "

Rani interrupted and said " This is the reason you must not marry a movie freak."

I said " Nisha. Ignore her and shoot her."

" Are you trying to make me a murderer? "

" Nope. Listen to me then at least. I will tell the truth."

I tried hard to convince her. I said " You have the gun. If you don't trust me you can shoot me. But before that allow me to tell the truth."

She said " Ok. Go ahead."

I told everything from my travel journey to Mahabaleshwar, the gangster I arranged and then ended by telling that the meat she ate was human flesh and not Buffalo flesh.

She vomited and said " What the fuck? I ate Human flesh. I am going to shoot you for this."

I replied " You said you loved it. I would have died if I didn't do that. I did those for my survival. I never killed anyone. I just ate those who were already dead."

She said " But you tried to kill me."

" No I didn't."

I looked at Rani and threw the bottle she gave me on her. It passed through her.

I asked " Did you see that Nisha? Bottle went through her."

She was more afraid now. She said " What the fuck again? I am between a ghost and a cannibal monster."

I said " Just a cannibal and not a monster. But she is a ghost."

She said " What? Are you joking at this moment? "

Rani said " What the fuck? You are making a serious thriller moment into a funny moment."

Nisha said " But I don't trust you. "

Rani said " Then shoot him."

I said " Please Nisha. Don't listen to her. All I needed was a little flesh from you to cure this disease."

She asked " So you loved me and married me just for my flesh. Am I right? "

I shouted " No no no. She said very late that the solution is you for my problem."

She pointed the gun towards Rani and asked " Who the hell are you? Why are you doing this?"

Rani answered " There is no point in pointing a gun at me. But still I will talk to you."

" I am Rani. That's all I can tell about myself. But this man Yoga is a cannibal by birth. I never placed cannibalism inside him. All I did was just trigger it. That's all. I just brought out what was inside him. Normally people kill each other when I do this. But this man never killed anyone. So I gave him a solution. That was you. Even then he never thought of killing you. He loves you a lot. So I am thinking of healing him for you. "

I said " What? Now you are turning out to be a good ghost."

Nisha shouted " Listen to her. She will cure you."

I still doubted Rani because she can manipulate me and get me into another trouble.

While I was thinking, someone opened the door rapidly and accidentally hit me. Nisha, the moment she saw it, pulled the trigger of the gun. The gun shot the man who opened the door. He fell on me and when I turned him back and saw, it was Ravi.

I shouted " Oh my god. You killed someone."

Nisha fainted as soon as she knew she murdered someone.

I looked towards Rani and asked " Can you help me please?"

She agreed and said " Yes."

I thought " Why the hell did he come now at the wrong time? "

Rani used her magic to clean the blood. Before that I cut the flesh into multiple pieces, I am expert in that. Then I packed and kept it in the refrigerator. I collected the bones and buried them in the cemetery which I visited earlier before someone noticed me.

Then I came back home and started cooking different recipes with the flesh I had. I picked Nisha and placed her on the bed. I asked Rani " Is there any magic you can do to erase these moments from her brain?"

She said " I will try."

" Please do it."

She said " Ok." She moved her hands and did something. She said " When she wakes up, she won't remember anything that happened that night."

" Thank you Rani."

She asked " What did you do with the gun? "

I said " I dug it along with the bones in the graveyard."

She said " Okay. It's time for me to leave."

I thanked her again and she vanished forever from my life. Then I was waiting till the morning. Nisha woke up. I was afraid whether she would remember everything or not. She came and said " Good morning. It was a deep sleep."

" Good morning."

I was relieved when I came to know that she didn't remember anything. She smelled the kitchen and found loads of food prepared.

She asked, " You were busy all night cooking."

" Yes. I prayed to God that I will give food to the old age home once we get married. That's why I started preparing the food for them."

She said " The smell is good. Shall I taste it?"

" No. Please no. I have other plans for us today at Hilton hotel."

She said " It's good. You are a man of lots of surprises. "

Then I started packing the foods in the plastic boxes which I brought from the nearby store. Nisha joined me and helped me. Then I packed those boxes in two bags and booked an auto.

She asked, " What about the remaining food?"

I said, " You know what to do."

I told her and left for the old age home to deliver the food. She gave the remaining food to neighbour Rishi. Then the remaining food to the street dogs. Once the job was done, I took Nisha to the Hilton Hotel for lunch.

I asked " What would you like to have? "

She said " Irish Whiskey."

I requested two Irish whiskey. They brought traditional glasses. We both took a glass of whiskey and said " Cheers."

POST CLIMAX

Those men who were stealing dead bodies from the cemetery were digging a grave that night. They found only a human skull and a gun.

One of them said " It's a gun."

They all looked at each other. A man said " There is another cannibal in the town just like us."

Another guy said " Definitely it's the same person whom we were chasing that day. We need to find him."

The first person said " We haven't seen him."

" Let's inform the boss regarding this."

Printed by Libri Plureos GmbH in Hamburg,
Germany